Farmyard Tales

The Grumpy Goat

Heather Amery

Illustrated by Stephen Cartwright

Adapted by Lara Bryan

Reading consultant: Alison Kelly

Find the duck on every double page.

This story is about Apple Tree Farm,

Sam,

Poppy,

Ted,

Rusty

and Gertie,
the goat.

One morning, Ted
asked Poppy and Sam
to clean the goat shed.

Sam was worried...

Poppy and Sam went
into the goat pen.

Gertie pushed Sam over.

They shut the gate.

"I have an idea,"
said Sam.

Sam tried to tempt
Gertie out with bread.

Gertie stayed in her pen.

Poppy dropped some
grass by the gate.

Gertie still stayed
in her pen.

"I have another idea,"
said Sam.

"I'll dress up as Ted.
Gertie likes Ted."

Sam dressed up in
Ted's clothes.

Gertie wasn't fooled. She
pushed Sam over again.

Then they tried to catch
Gertie with a rope.

Gertie chased them...

...and ran out of her pen.

Finally, Poppy and Sam
could clean Gertie's shed.

Then they let
her back in.

The next morning,
Ted took them back
to the pen.

Gertie had a baby!

Sam laughed. "She doesn't look grumpy anymore."

Puzzles

Puzzle 1

Put these pictures in the right order to tell the story.

A.

B.

C.

D.

E.

Puzzle 2

Who's who? Match the names to the people or animals in this story.

Gertie

Ted

Rusty

Poppy

Sam

Puzzle 3

Can you spot five differences
between these two pictures?

Puzzle 4

Choose the missing word for each picture.

catch   pushed   ran

A.

Gertie _____ Sam over.

B.

They tried to _____ Gertie.

C.

Gertie _____ out.

Answers to puzzles
Puzzle 1

1D.

2A.

3C.

4E.

5B.

Puzzle 2

Sam

Poppy

Ted

Rusty

Gertie

Puzzle 3

Puzzle 4

A.
Gertie
<u>pushed</u>
Sam over.

B.
They tried
to <u>catch</u>
Gertie.

C.
Gertie
<u>ran</u> out.

Designed by Laura Nelson
Digital manipulation by Nick Wakeford

This edition first published in 2017 by Usborne Publishing Ltd.,
Usborne House, 83-85 Saffron Hill, London EC1N 8RT, England.
www.usborne.com Copyright © 2017, 1989 Usborne Publishing Ltd.

USBORNE FIRST READING
Level Two Farmyard Tales

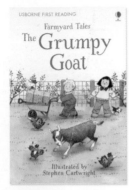

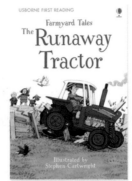

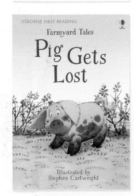

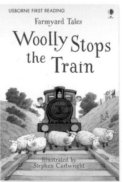

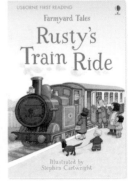